Have fun
we love
you!!

Presented To

Amanda

From

Aunt Sherry & Uncle Dave

Aug 24   19 _98_

Dear Parents:

Regular checkups are an important part of your child's ongoing health care. These visits allow your child's doctor to perform a complete physical exam; discuss topics such as nutrition, development, behavior, and safety; answer questions you may have; and administer appropriate vaccinations.

These doctor visits may be stressful for some children, and your child's anxiety may make the checkup more difficult. Try reading this book to your child before a scheduled visit to the doctor. Your child may have a better understanding about what to expect and thus be less anxious.

Russell McDonald, M.D., F.A.A.P.
Pediatrician

Art Director: Tricia Legault
Designer: Hilarie Brannan Ireton

©1996 The Lyons Group

PUBLISHING
300 East Bethany Drive, Allen, Texas 75002

    6 7 8 9 10   99 98 97

ISBN 1-57064-074-2

Library of Congress Number 95-79188

Go To The Doctor

Written by Margie Larsen, M.Ed.
Photography by Dennis Full

Baby Bop is going to the doctor for her checkup. "It's been one year since you had your last checkup," says Barney.

"I-I'm a little scared," says Baby Bop.

"I know," says Barney. "Going to the doctor can be scary. But remember, doctors are our friends. They help people stay healthy."

Robert Russell, M.D.
Pediatrician

At the doctor's office, Baby Bop sees Julie the nurse. "Hi, Baby Bop. It's good to see you again."

"I'm here for my checkup. What is a checkup?" asks Baby Bop.

"A checkup," says nurse Julie, "is when the doctor examines or checks you from your head to your toes."

"He wants to make sure you're strong and healthy," says Barney.

The doctor comes in to see Baby Bop.
She thinks her doctor is very nice.
"How are you doing?" asks Dr. Russell.

"I'm strong and healthy," says Baby Bop.

First, nurse Julie and Dr. Russell weigh Baby Bop on a scale. Then they measure her height to see how much she has grown.

"Look, I'm a big girl now!" says Baby Bop.

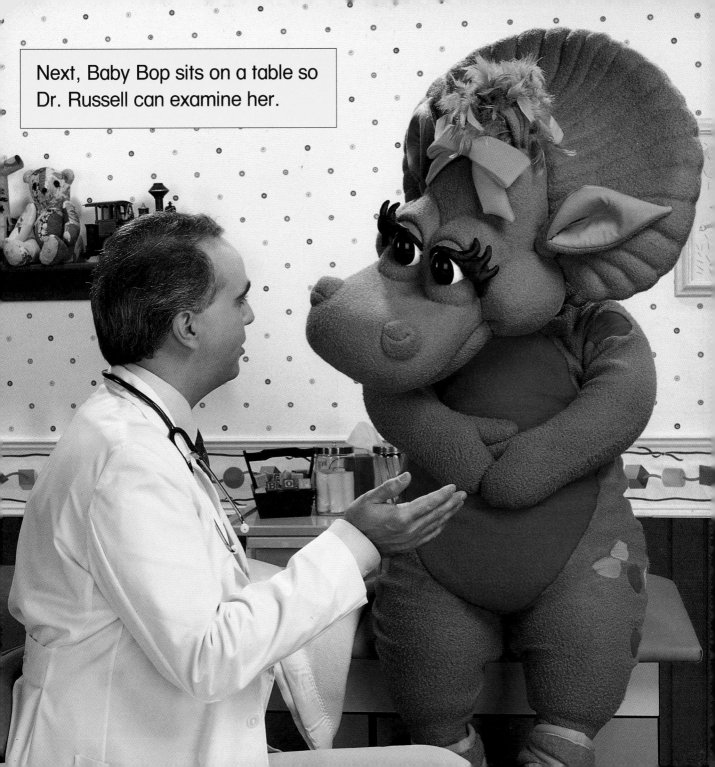

Next, Baby Bop sits on a table so Dr. Russell can examine her.

"Open wide and say ahhhh," says Dr. Russell.

"Ahhhh," says Baby Bop.

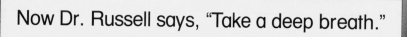
Now Dr. Russell says, "Take a deep breath."

Baby Bop takes a deep breath. "Good job, Baby Bop."

"I need to listen to your heartbeat," says Dr. Russell. "The stethoscope may feel cold."

Baby Bop hears her heartbeat, too.
"Ker-thump, ker-thump, ker-thump!"

Dr. Russell looks at her eyes and inside her ears.
"That tickles," says Baby Bop with a giggle.

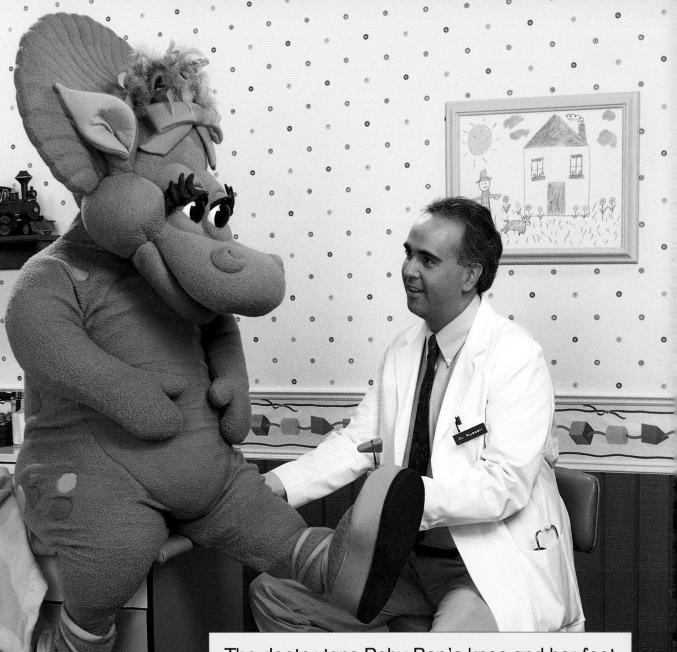

The doctor taps Baby Bop's knee and her foot jumps up! "That felt funny," says Baby Bop.

"You were a good patient, Baby Bop, and you are strong and healthy. I'm glad you came to see me today," says Dr. Russell.

"I'm glad I came, too!" says Baby Bop.

"Going to the doctor isn't so scary, Barney. Doctors help people stay healthy!"